BOYSRULE!

Halloween Gotcha!

Felice Arena and Phil Kettle

illustrated by
Gus Go

RISING ★ STARS

First published in Great Britain by
RISING STARS UK LTD 2005
76 Farnaby Road, Bromley, BR1 4BH

For information visit our website at:
www.risingstars-uk.com

British Library Cataloguing in Publication Data

A CIP record for this book is available from the British Library.

ISBN: 1-905056-13-3

First published in 2004 by
MACMILLAN EDUCATION AUSTRALIA PTY LTD
627 Chapel Street, South Yarra, Australia 3141

Visit our website at www.macmillan.com.au

Associated companies and representatives throughout the world.

Project Management by Limelight Press Pty Ltd
Cover and text design by Lore Foye
Illustrations by Gus Gordon

Printed and bound in Great Britain by
Mackays of Chatham plc, Chatham, Kent

BOYS RULE!

Contents

CHAPTER 1
October's Last, Best Day   1

CHAPTER 2
Itsy Bitsy Spider   7

CHAPTER 3
Zombie Warning   13

CHAPTER 4
Blood-sucking Beetles   20

CHAPTER 5
Scared to Death   25

EXTRA STUFF

• **Halloween Lingo**   33

• **Halloween Must-dos**   34

• **Halloween Instant Info**   36

• **Think Tank**   38

• **Hi Guys! (Author Letter)**   40

• **When We Were Kids**   42

• **What a Laugh!**   43

Sam   Billy

CHAPTER 1

October's Last, Best Day

Sam is in the hallway of his house, staring at himself in the mirror. He is dressed in a Dracula costume waiting patiently for his friend Billy to arrive. It is Halloween and they've arranged to go trick or treating together. It's also Sam's birthday.

Sam "My name is Count Drac-u-la! Ha, ha, ha. I want to suck your blood! Ha, ha, ha."

There's a knock at the front door. Sam opens it and is shocked to see Billy wearing a dress and a wig.

Sam "Arggh! A girl! What? Why?"

Billy "Mum forgot to pick up my werewolf costume. And then we didn't have enough time to find anything else. So, I thought, 'Well, what's just as scary as a werewolf?' Then it suddenly came to me—my sister! Cool, huh?"

Sam "I don't believe it! Maybe I can find another set of vampire teeth and a cape for you ... or an old bed sheet and we can cut out the eyes and you can go as a ghost."

Billy "No, it's cool. It's not that bad, really. You know, I didn't think wearing a dress could be so comfortable."

Sam "Now you're *really* scaring me."

Billy "Oh yeah, I nearly forgot, Happy Birthday. I bought something for you."

Sam "Thanks!"

Sam rips open the present and discovers an empty bug catcher.

Sam "Um, thanks … I think."

Billy "Arr, no! It's escaped!"

Sam "What's escaped?"

Billy "Your gift. I remembered how you said you'd found your pet tarantula, Spike, dead in your terrarium the other day. So I got you a new one. And now it's gone!"

Sam suddenly spots a huge black
hairy tarantula crawling on the
top of Billy's wig.

Sam "Um, I don't think so."

CHAPTER 2

Itsy Bitsy Spider

Sam's eyes fix on the spider. His look makes Billy think he could be in trouble.

Sam "Don't move an inch. It's crawling on your head."
Billy "My head!"

Sam "I said, don't move. You don't want it sinking its fangs into your skull, do you?"

Billy "What are you going to do?"

Sam steps towards Billy. He gently raises the bug catcher over the spider.

Sam (whispering) "Don't ... move."

Billy closes his eyes, too scared to watch. Sam moves the bug catcher away from Billy's head again.

Sam "Easy now, can't rush it."

Billy "Will you hurry up! I'm going to be attacked any second."

Sam "Look out!"

Billy "What?"

Sam "No. False alarm. It looked like it was going to bite you, that's all."

Billy "Oh great, I'm going to die now. Sam, if this thing kills me, you can have my new football. And my baseball bat."

Sam "What about your Game Boy?"

Billy "Sam!"

Sam "OK, OK! Right, just a little closer now."

Sam suddenly swoops the bug catcher on top of the spider, quickly scooping it inside. Billy lets out a huge sigh of relief. Sam runs upstairs to his bedroom and drops the spider into his terrarium. As he leaves his room, he sees a plastic spider sitting on his chest of drawers and slips it into his pocket. It could come in handy tonight, he thinks. Moments later, Sam's back with Billy.

Sam "You were so scared. You should've seen your face! What a wimp!"

Billy "Yeah, we'll see how brave you are tonight. It's Halloween remember—anything can happen."

Billy lets out an over-the-top, scary laugh—like a villain in a movie.

Sam "See, that just doesn't work in a dress. Let's go trick or treating."

CHAPTER 3

Zombie Warning

Sam, Billy and Sam's father join a
parade of kids and parents walking
around their neighbourhood. A
stream of vampires, witches, ghosts
and superheroes is moving from
house to house, trick or treating.

Sam "That place was a good one. Check out all the sweets I got."

Sam and Billy are using pillowcases to collect their treats. The boys compare what they've collected so far.

Billy "I went to that house over there and got about ten bars of chocolate. The owner was dressed as a zombie. He looked really cool. He had fake blood coming out of his ears."

Sam "Cool!"

Billy "But then he said something weird to me."

Sam "What?"

Billy "Well, apart from saying he thought I was a pretty little girl and that it was a shame I didn't have a costume, he also said that if we want to find the best sweets ever—like a whole truck load—we should go to that old house at the end of the street."

Sam "But that house is empty. No-one's lived there for months. And I've heard it's haunted too."

Billy "I know. But the zombie said the last person who lived there owned a sweet shop. And he hid a lot of stuff in his house."

Sam "I don't know ... "

Sam's father calls out to Sam and Billy that he has to go home for a minute or two. He's just had a call on his phone and it's business. He tells the boys to go ahead and that he'll catch up with them later.

Billy "Perfect. Now we can go and check out the house."

Sam "I said, *I don't think so.*"

Billy "Don't tell me you're chicken!"

Sam "Yeah, right. You can't talk. Look who thought he was going to be killed by a spider. You *girl*!"

Billy "Well, what's your problem then? Let's go!"

Sam "Okay! Let's go."

CHAPTER 4

Blood-sucking Beetles

Billy and Sam separate from the other trick or treaters and head towards the empty house. The end of the street is darker and more deserted as they approach the eerie looking, run-down building. They are the only ones around ... or are they?

Sam "Maybe we should head back?"

Billy "No way! We're almost there."

Sam "But what if ... ?"

Billy "But what if, what?"

Sam "What if there's something living there?"

Billy "Like what?"

Sam "Like, I dunno. Flesh-eating ghosts maybe."

Billy "I don't think so. Ghosts can't eat you."

Sam "Okay, but what about if there's a million blood-sucking beetles that come out of the cracks in the floor and eat you alive in 30 seconds?"

Billy "Cut it out, will you! Now you're freaking me out."

Billy and Sam reach the old gate to the house. The cold-looking building is lit up by the full moon in the sky.

Sam "This is crazy. And how are we going to find anything in the dark?"

Billy "Relax, will you!"

Sam "Hey! I just saw a light turn on and off in that window upstairs. Someone's inside."

Billy "Well, I didn't see it. You sure?"

Sam "Yes! Let's forget the sweets. We've got enough."

Billy "Gee, you're a chicken. Come on, we'll just take a peek. And besides, you're Dracula. This is the type of place Dracula would live in."

Sam "That's what I'm afraid of."

Billy walks up the path to the house. Sam nervously follows.

CHAPTER 5

Scared to Death

The boys reach the front door and discover that it's unlocked. The door makes a creaking sound when Billy pushes it open.

Billy "Hello? Anyone there?"

Sam "I can't believe we're doing this. We're going to die. Please don't kill us, blood-sucking beetles."

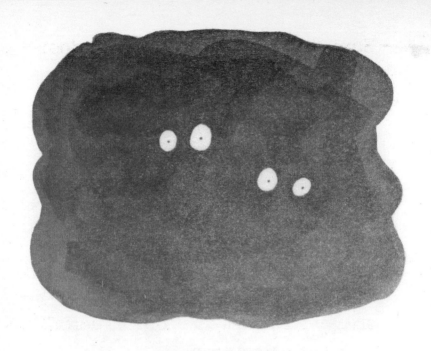

The boys walk into the large, pitch black hallway. Suddenly, from out of nowhere, something whizzes past Sam's leg.

Sam "ARRGGGHH!!"
Billy "ARRGGGHH what? What is it?"
Sam "Run! I'm being attacked!"
Billy "No, wait. Look, it's just a cat."

Sam looks back out the front door and sees a stray black cat dashing across the lawn.

Billy "Are you okay?"

Sam "I'm about to wet myself! I'm *really* busting. Let's go, Billy. Sorry if I called you a wimp and teased you about the spider. This is really creepy now. Let's get out of here."

Billy "Look up there! At the top of the stairs. There's a light on. You were right, someone is here."

Sam "See! So come on, let's go then. Billy!"

Billy ignores Sam and begins to walk upstairs. Sam shakes his head, annoyed with his friend. He reluctantly follows.

Sam (whispering) "You're nuts, Billy. My dad is probably looking for us. I can just see it. In a few minutes all he'll be able to find will be our skeletons. And then *he'll* be attacked by the beetles or whoever or whatever is up there."

Billy and Sam reach the top of
the staircase and sneak towards the
lit-up room. The boys slowly walk
in and suddenly: "*Surprise!!! Happy
birthday Sam!*"

Sam is scared out of his skin.
Standing there are his entire family
and some of his friends from school.

Sam (trying to catch his breath)
"You mean this was all a set-up?
For my birthday?"
Billy (chuckling) "Yep—it was all my
idea. And we got you a good one!"

Sam quickly reaches into his pocket and pulls out the plastic black spider. He throws it towards Billy's face. Billy jumps back and screams. Everyone laughs— especially Sam.

Sam "Gotcha back! And thanks, this is the coolest birthday surprise ever!"

Sam

BOYS RULE!

Halloween Lingo

Billy

Halloween A celebration held on 31 October, the day before All Saint's Day. Kids (and adults) go door to door in the evening, wearing costumes and asking for treats or playing tricks.

scared When you're afraid.

tarantula A large, hairy spider that can give you a painful bite but not kill you.

vampire A fictional character that rises from the grave at night to suck the blood of sleeping people.

werewolf A monster able to change its appearance from a human to a wolf.

Halloween Must-dos

☞ Plan your costume at least a week before Halloween. You don't want to be looking for one or making it at the last minute.

☞ Whenever you laugh, try to make it sound really evil—like a villain in a movie.

☞ Try not to bite anyone with your plastic fang teeth. You could make an awful mess, and it's not polite!

☞ Always tells scary ghost stories when it's dark outside—it's scarier that way.

☞ Never go trick or treating without a parent or guardian—you need someone to hold all the sweets you're going to get!

☞ Never take unwrapped or unsealed sweets from anyone—you don't know where they've come from. Yuck, gross!

☞ Don't eat all your treats in one night or you'll be ill and want to throw up. It might look like green smelly, pea and ham soup—now that's scary!

☞ Help your parents to carve out a pumpkin to make a jack-o'-lantern to use as a Halloween decoration.

Halloween Instant Info

The most famous vampire is Dracula. The character was created by Irish writer, Bram Stoker.

The character of Dracula has appeared in 162 films.

Some people believe that Halloween first began 2000 years ago as a part of an ancient Celtic festival which celebrated the new year on 1 November.

The official colours of Halloween are orange and black.

The most jack-o'-lanterns lit at one time were 23 727 on 28 October 2000 at the Keene Pumpkin Festival, New Hampshire, USA.

The largest sweet counter in the world is at the Chutter General Store in Littleton, New Hampshire, USA. It measures 34.11 metres in length. An awful lot of sweets could fit on that counter!

Pumpkins are really popular for cooking around Halloween time— the largest pumpkin pie ever baked weighed 15.75 kilograms and was 1.5 metres in diameter.

Think Tank

1 When is Halloween celebrated?

2 What are the official colours of Halloween?

3 What sort of lantern can you make with a pumpkin?

4 What is a vampire's favourite pastime?

5 What do you get to eat a lot of at Halloween?

6 Which animal do witches like?

7 What's scarier—a blood-sucking zombie or a headless ghost?

8 How many legs does a tarantula have?

Answers

8 It's a spider, so it has eight legs.

7 I don't know. I wouldn't hang around long enough to find out, so both are right—a free point.

6 A cat is a witch's best friend, usually it's a black one.

5 You get a lot of sweets (and a bellyache) at Halloween.

4 Sucking blood is a vampire's favourite pastime.

3 You can make a jack-o'-lantern from a pumpkin.

2 The official colours of Halloween are black and orange.

1 Halloween is on 31 October.

How did you score?

- If you got all 8 answers correct you're a scare freak. Halloween is your favourite day of the year.

- If you got 6 answers correct, then you like to be scared but prefer to eat a truck load of sweets if given the choice.

- If you got fewer than 4 answers correct, then you're a real scaredy cat—you probably sleep with the light on! Halloween might not be for you.

Felice →

← Phil

Hi Guys!

We have heaps of fun reading and want you to, too. We both believe that being a good reader is really important and so cool.

Try out our suggestions to help you have fun as you read.

At school, why don't you use "Halloween Gotcha!" as a play and you and your friends can be the actors. Set the scene for your play. Bring some suitable things to school for a halloween costume and a pumpkin for a jack-o'-lantern. If you can't manage a pumpkin, use your acting skills and imagination to pretend.

So ... have you decided who is going to be Sam and who is going to be Billy? Now, with your friends, read and act out our story in front of the class.

We have a lot of fun when we go to schools and read our stories. After we finish the kids all clap really loudly. When you've finished your play your classmates will do the same. Just remember to look out the window—there might be a talent scout from a television station watching you!

Reading at home is really important and a lot of fun as well.

Take our books home and get someone in your family to read them with you. Maybe they can take on a part in the story.

Remember, reading is a whole lot of fun.

So, as the frog in the local pond would say, Read-it!

And remember, Boys Rule!

Felice

When We Were Kids

Phil

Phil "When I was a kid, horror movies used to scare me. I'd have nightmares."

Felice "Yes? How often?"

Phil "All the time. One day I dreamt I heard knocking at my bedroom window. It was very dark and scary."

Felice "What did you do? Hide under the covers?"

Phil "No, I got up and went over to the window, pulled back the curtain and …"

Felice "And what? What was it?"

Phil "Come closer. It was a … RAARGH!"

Felice "ARRGGGHHHHHH!!"

Phil "Gotcha!"

BOYS RULE!
What a Laugh!

Q What do ghosts serve for pudding?

A I scream.

BOYS RULE!

| Gone Fishing | The Tree House | Golf Legends | Camping Out | Bike Daredevils |

| Water Rats | Skateboard Dudes | Tennis Ace | Basketball Buddies | Secret Agent Heroes |

| Wet World | Rock Star | Pirate Attack | Olympic Champions | Race Car Dreamers |

| Hit the Beach | Rotten School Day | Halloween Gotcha! | Battle of the Games | On the Farm |

44